KU-515-104

This Orchard book

belongs to

_____

_____

_____

With love and
thanks to Nat.
Giles

For Justin
the best daddy
in the world.
Emma x

ORCHARD BOOKS

338 Euston Road, London NW1 3BH

Orchard Books Australia

Level 17/207 Kent Street, Sydney, NSW 2000

First published in 2011 by Orchard Books

First published in paperback in 2012

ISBN 978 1 40831 301 5

Text © Giles Andreae 2011

Illustrations © Emma Dodd 2011

The rights of Giles Andreae to be identified as the author
and of Emma Dodd to be identified as the illustrator
of this work has been asserted by them in accordance
with the Copyright, Designs and Patents Act, 1988.

A CIP catalogue record for this book
is available from the British Library.

10 9 8 7 6 5 4 3 2 1

Printed in China

Orchard Books is a division
of Hachette Children's Books,
an Hachette UK Company.

www.hachette.co.uk

I love my daddy

Giles Andreae
& Emma Dodd

ORCHARD

I love my daddy, yes I do,

He's very kind – and funny too.

He teaches loads of things to me,

I think he's clever. So does he!

He lets me clamber on his back,

And we play horsies – click clack clack.

He sings me all his favourite songs,

I love to dance and sing along.

His shoes are very big and brown,

They make me look a real clown!

He lifts me on his shoulders high,

Until I nearly touch the sky.

And when we're playing on the swings,
He does all sorts of silly things.

For treats, when mummy's not at home,

We sometimes watch TV alone!

And when it's time to eat my tea,

He always says, "One bite for me?"

I really love to cuddle him,

And feel the prickles on his chin.

He tucks me safely into bed,
Then tells me stories from his head.

My daddy's such a lovely man,

In fact, I am his BIGGEST fan!